SLEEPY RIVER

HANNA BANDES

illustrated by JEANETTE WINTER

Philomel Books ✒ New York

Philomel Books, a division of The Putnam & Grosset Group, 200 Madison Avenue, New York, NY 10016.
Published simultaneously in Canada. Printed in Hong Kong by South China Printing Co. (1988) Ltd.
Book design by Gunta Alexander. The text is set in Hiroshige.
Library of Congress Cataloging-in-Publication Data
Bandes, Hanna. Sleepy river / by Hanna Bandes; illustrated by Jeanette Winter.
p.   cm.   Summary: A canoe ride at nightfall provides a mother and child
glimpses of ducks, fireflies, bats, and other wonders of nature.
[1. Nature—Fiction. 2. Animals—Fiction. 3. Night—Fiction.]   I. Winter, Jeanette, ill.
II. Title.   PZ7.B2212S1   1993   [E]—dc20   92-26198   CIP   AC
ISBN 0-399-22349-5
1 3 5 7 9 10 8 6 4 2
First Impression

In memory of Mildred and Merrill Munger,
who taught me to appreciate the natural world. —H.B.

"Come watch the night fall, small one,"

says Mother with a smile.

The sleek canoe slides from the sand
into the shade near the shore.

Splish, splish, splish, says the paddle.
Hush-h-h-h, says the canoe in the silvery water.

Ducklings and ducks
in the deepening dark
dip and dive for dinner.

Heron stands like a hero
high on the bank,
then flies on huge wings home.

Dainty deer drink at dusk.

Sun slips away.

Fireflies flicker in the fading light.

Stately sycamores solemnly stand,
silhouettes on a scarlet sky.

Darkness descends.

Little brown bats,
in a silent ballet,
bob in the balmy night breeze.

Raccoon runs along the riverbank.

Whoo, whoo, whoo's on my river?
Whoo? asks the haughty hoot owl.

Moon's a silver circle,
serene in the summer sky.

Shooting star speeds away.

Luminous lacewings lift from the water,
lightly landing on lily pads.

Plop! jumps a fish,
and sparkly circles spread to the shore.
Placid luna moth passes.

Milky Way is a magical maze.

Moonbeam makes a mystical path
marking the way back home.

Splish, says the peaceful paddle.
Hush-h-h-h, says the canoe in the silvery water.

Back home, a bright light beckons.

The sleek canoe slips to the shore,
stars sing a silent symphony.

And small one's sound asleep.